KATE SALLEY PALMER

A GRACIOUS PLENTY

SIMON & SCHUSTER BOOKS FOR YOUNG READERS

Published by Simon & Schuster

New York • London • Toronto • Sydney • Tokyo • Singapore

SIMON & SCHUSTER BOOKS FOR YOUNG READERS

Simon & Schuster Building, Rockefeller Center, 1230 Avenue of the Americas, New York, New York 10020. Copyright © 1991 by Kate Salley Palmer. All rights reserved including the right of reproduction in whole or in part in any form. SIMON & SCHUSTER BOOKS FOR YOUNG READERS is a trademark of Simon & Schuster.

Designed by Lucille Chomowicz.
The text of this book is set in Kennerly.
The illustrations were done in colored pencil.
Manufactured in the United States of America.   10   9   8   7   6   5   4   3   2   1

Library of Congress Cataloging-in-Publication Data. Palmer, Kate Salley. A gracious plenty / by Kate Salley Palmer. Summary: Although she never married, Great-aunt May had a full life with children, friends, children, travel, and children—a life of gracious plenty.   [1. Great-aunts—Fiction.] I. Title.   PZ7.P18554Gr   1991   [E]—dc20   91-6485   AC   ISBN: 0-671-73566-7

For May, of course, and for Daddy, who probably thought I wasn't paying attention — KSP

M y great-aunt May never got married.
She never had children. She lived all by herself.

She had a couch covered in horsehair that scratched when you sat on it wearing shorts.

She had a small oil painting of a house and a pond; the painted house was reflected in the painted water.

She had books everywhere. She had
a wall full of books that she let us read
whenever we wanted.

She had pencils and pens and drawing
paper that we could use if we asked.

She had a bedroom fragrant with sweet-
smelling powder and magnolia blossoms.

She had real hairpins on her dresser, and a
silver brush and comb.

She had a big, sunny kitchen with a tiny refrigerator and a tiny stove.

She had dainty feet and wore modest, lace-up shoes with thick high heels—black in winter, white in summer.

She had a doorbell that was too loud, because she was hard of hearing.

She had a bathtub with feet.

She had a bottle of sherry wine and some little glasses—just for guests.

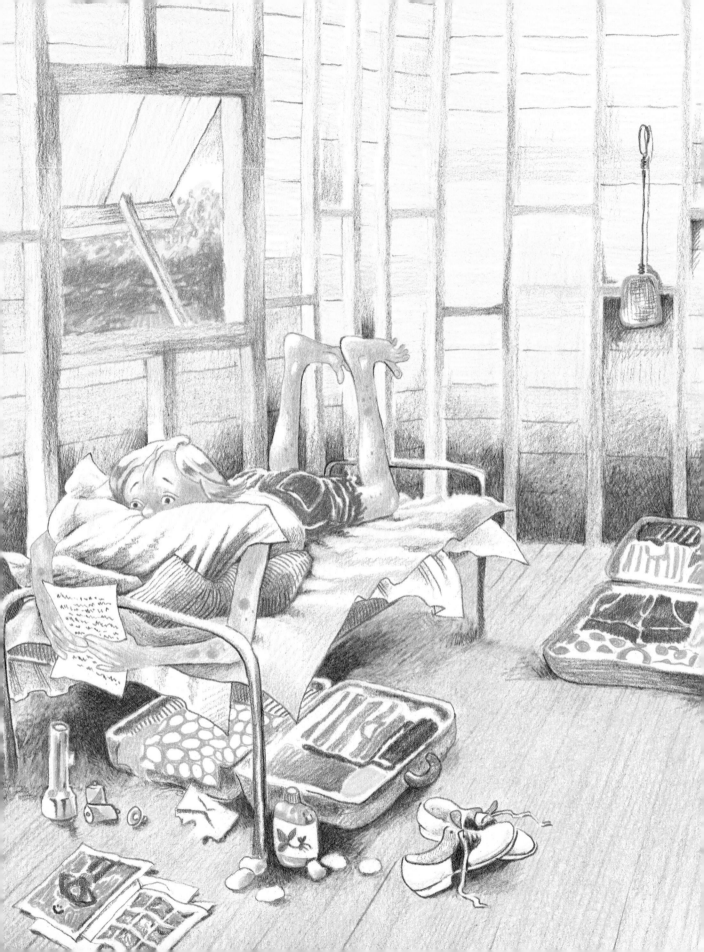

She had lots of letters to write—especially
when we were at summer camp.

She had dinner with us every Sunday
after church.

She had a nap every Sunday after dinner.

She had my father, her nephew, to drive her to the doctor and to the store.

She had pretty, wavy gray hair and a twinkly smile.

She had to laugh the day my baby brother
accidentally cussed at the dinner table.

She had amazing things to tell us—all of them true.

She had lots of people to miss her when she went away and to be glad when she came home.

She had, she said, a gracious plenty.